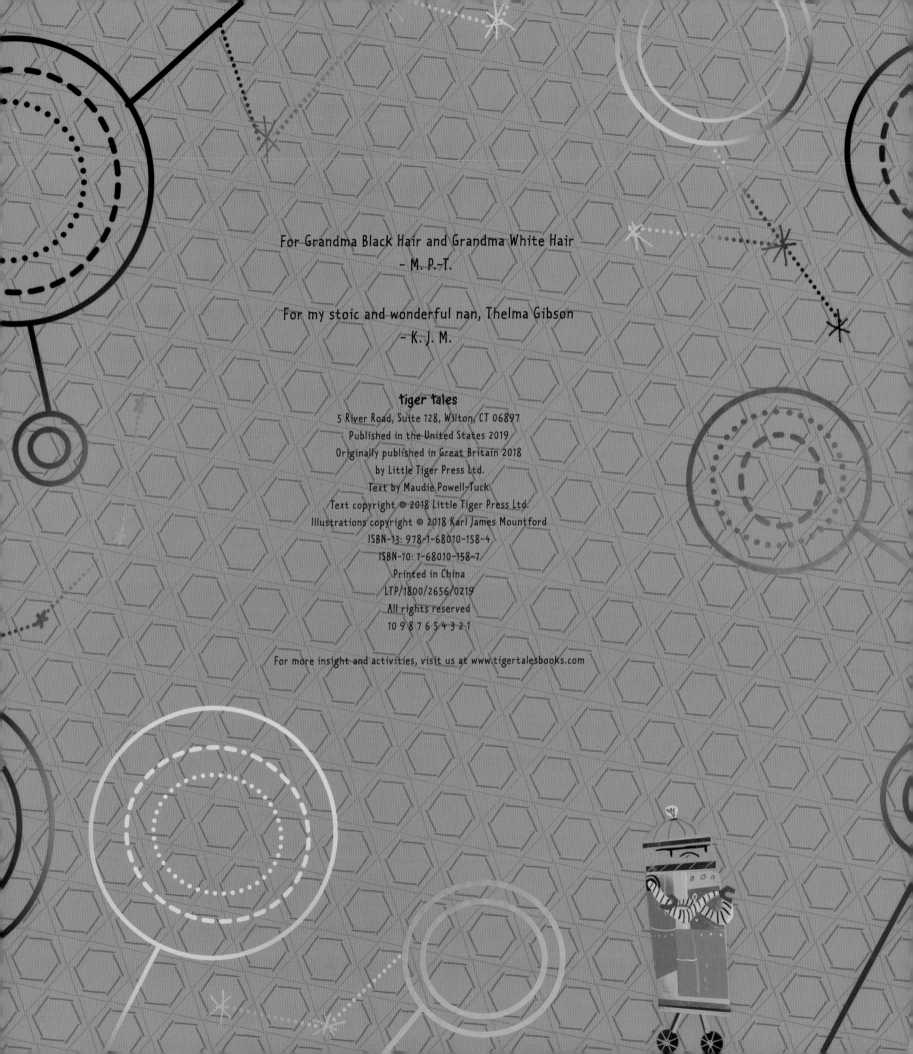

For Grandma Black Hair and Grandma White Hair
– M. P.-T.

For my stoic and wonderful nan, Thelma Gibson
– K. J. M.

**tiger tales**
5 River Road, Suite 128, Wilton, CT 06897
Published in the United States 2019
Originally published in Great Britain 2018
by Little Tiger Press Ltd.
Text by Maudie Powell-Tuck
Text copyright © 2018 Little Tiger Press Ltd.
Illustrations copyright © 2018 Karl James Mountford
ISBN-13: 978-1-68010-158-4
ISBN-10: 1-68010-158-7
Printed in China
LTP/1800/2656/0219

For more insight and activities, visit us at www.tigertalesbooks.com

# the SPACE TRAIN

by Maudie Powell-Tuck

Illustrated by Karl James Mountford

tiger tales

JAKOB'S LOG
04::01::2084
FORTUNA SPACE
STATION

Inventory 096:

1 Boy (me)

1 Grandma

1 Robot chicken
(Derek)

1 ToolBot (grumpy)

22 Abandoned airlocks

10 Deserted decks

54 Hangars
(12 unexplored)

1 Alien living in the
trash compactor

0 New friends

1 Mysterious thing
found (further
investigation needed)

Jakob lived light years from Earth,
in a space station on the edge of a galaxy.
He had a grandma, who would never sit still,
and a robot chicken named Derek.

Jakob also had a secret. Hidden away
in Hangar 19, he had found . . .

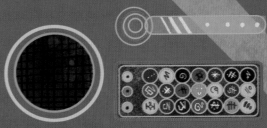

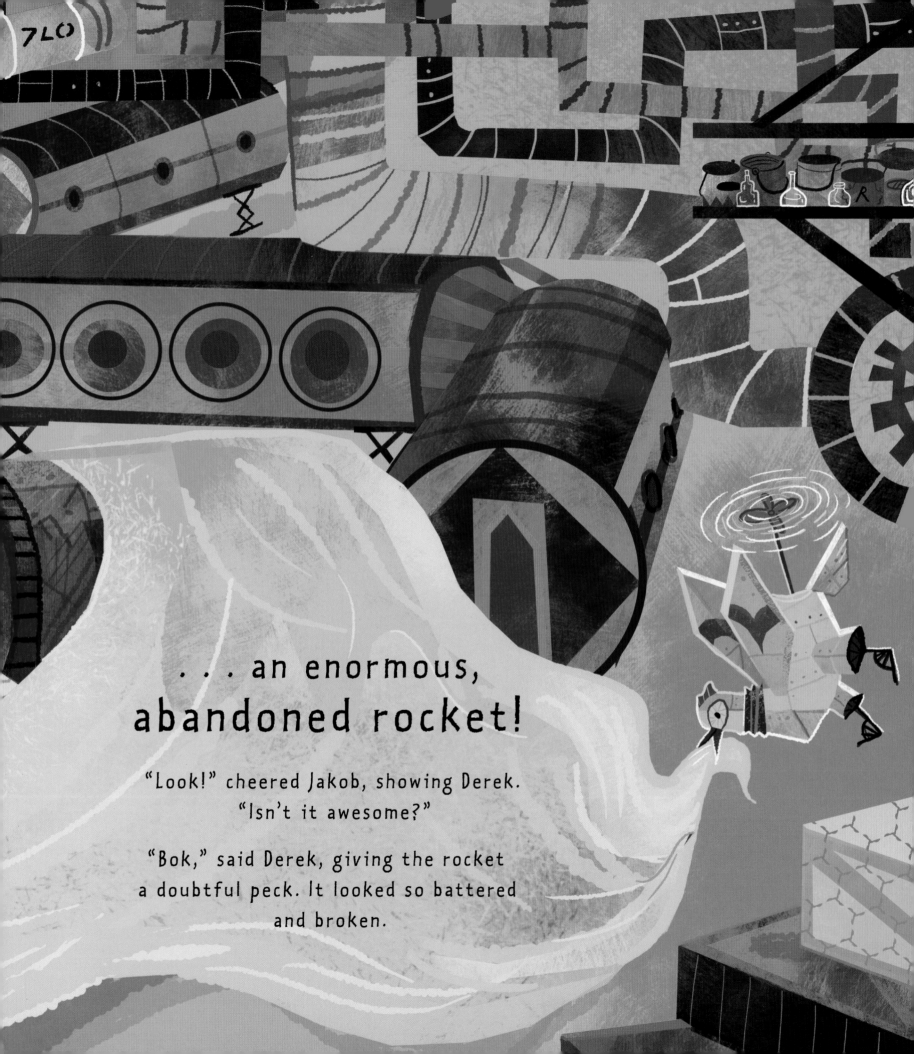

. . . an enormous,
**abandoned rocket!**

"Look!" cheered Jakob, showing Derek.
"Isn't it awesome?"

"Bok," said Derek, giving the rocket
a doubtful peck. It looked so battered
and broken.

But when Grandma saw the machine,
she danced on the spot.

"That's not a rusty rocket!
It's the SPACE TRAIN!"
she cried, so loudly that Derek
laid a screw in surprise.

"The Space Train?"
asked Jakob, wrinkling his nose.
"Bok?" clucked Derek.
Both were utterly baffled.

"When I was little," said Grandma, pulling out her holoprojector, "the Space Train crisscrossed the universe on tracks of stardust, visiting station after station—"

"How many stations?" interrupted Jakob, who liked facts and figures.

"Two thousand, seven hundred,
and forty-seven," Grandma replied.
"You could spend an entire year on the
train and not see them all."

"Wow!" cried Jakob. "Was the Space Train fast?"

"Faster than the fastest spaceship.
So fast it made the stars look
like streaks in the sky."

They creaked open a
door and climbed inside
the grand, dusty dining car.
"Who rode the train?" Jakob asked.

"All kinds of people,"
Grandma replied.
"Star explorers, comet
chasers, and time travelers.
There were artists and scientists,
too — and many, many children."

Children, thought Jakob.
They could be my friends. "Grandma,"
he said aloud. "We have to fix
this train!"

Then Derek laid nuts and bolts and anything else they might need . . .

. . . while Jakob went to find Grandma's ToolBot.

"I'm not coming," grumbled ToolBot. "I want to watch TV."
"Yes, you ARE," said Jakob, dragging him away.

Soon, everybody was ready.
"Let's begin," nodded Grandma.
"ToolBot, pass me a wrench."

They worked all week, riveting,
welding, and fixing.

Jakob heaved lost wheels back into place, while Derek hammered loose valves. Grandma whistled as she repaired the train's thrusters, and ToolBot sat around doing nothing.

"Almost done!" grinned Jakob as they
blast-cleaned the combustion chamber.
"Bok!" coughed Derek tiredly.

Finally, the train was ready.
"It's finished!" cheered Jakob, spinning Derek around.
"Can I watch TV now?" asked ToolBot.
"Bedtime," said Grandma firmly. "We'll launch the train in the morning."

That night, as a special treat, they slept out on the observation deck.

"Did you know that the Space Train can carry 200 passengers?" Jakob whispered to Derek as Grandma snored in her sleep pod.

## JAKOB'S LOG
04::08::2084
FORTUNA SPACE STATION

Top 3 people I want to meet on the Space Train:

1. A dinkybop (smallest creature in the universe!) from Planet Wooloo.

2. A star whale from the Flaming Moons of Kai.

3. Other boys and girls just like me.

P.S. I'm so excited!

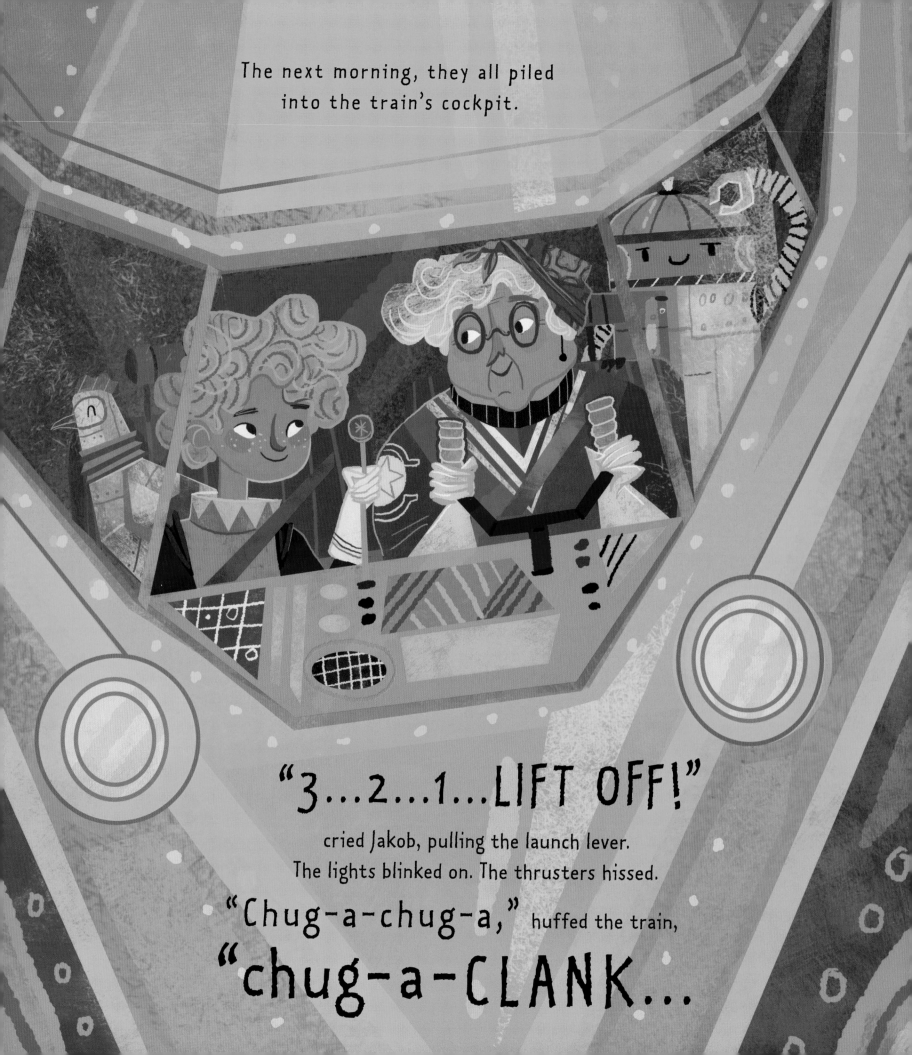

The next morning, they all piled
into the train's cockpit.

# "3...2...1...LIFT OFF!"

cried Jakob, pulling the launch lever.
The lights blinked on. The thrusters hissed.

## "Chug-a-chug-a," huffed the train,

# "chug-a-CLANK...

# BANG!!

"Silly train!" shouted Jakob.
"We did all that work for nothing!"

"SQUAWK!" wailed Derek.
Even ToolBot was a little disappointed.

Grandma gave them all a no-nonsense look.
"Everything can be fixed," she said firmly.
"Now don't just stand there like bottles of milk.
Find the problem and try again."

Derek checked the nuts and bolts, while Jakob pored over the engine plans.

"What's this here?" he said at last.

"Of course!" cried Grandma. "We forgot the blast rod."

So Derek squeezed out a blast rod, and ToolBot screwed it in place.

Then they all pulled the launch lever. "Please, please work!" willed Jakob.

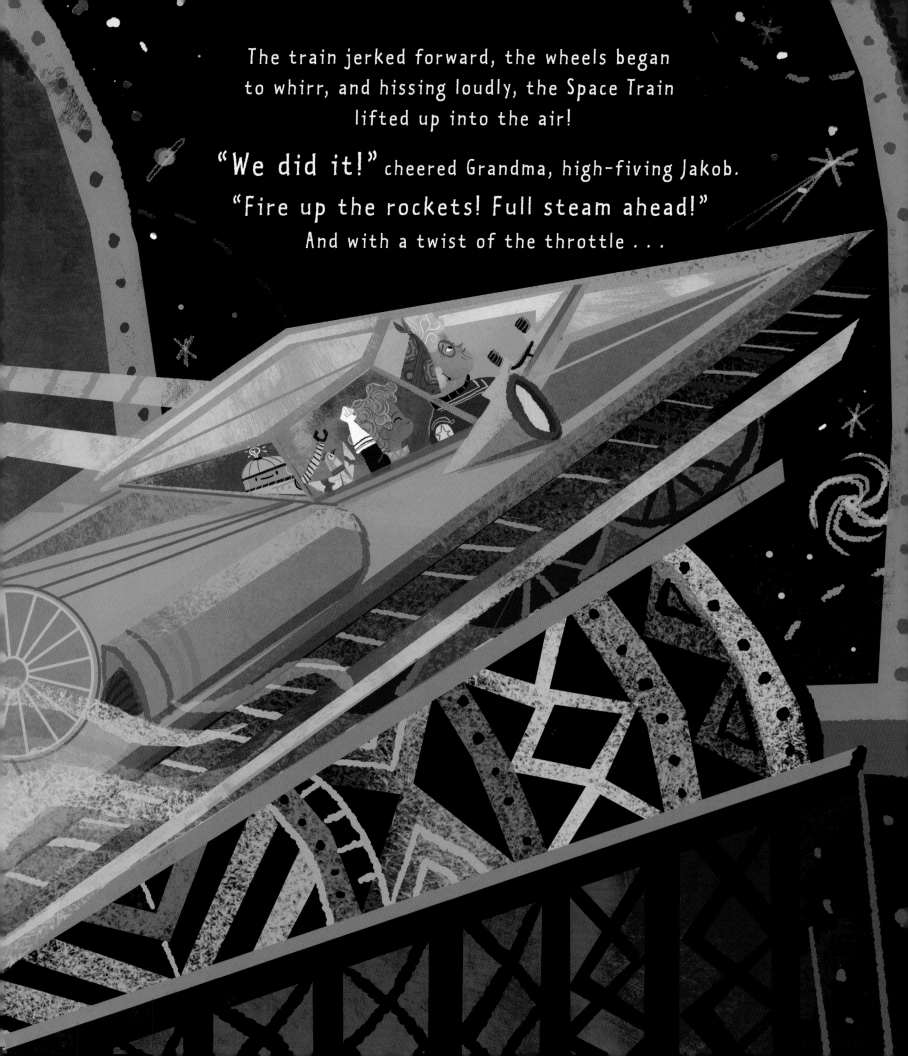

The train jerked forward, the wheels began
to whirr, and hissing loudly, the Space Train
lifted up into the air!

"We did it!" cheered Grandma, high-fiving Jakob.
"Fire up the rockets! Full steam ahead!"
And with a twist of the throttle . . .

. . . the train blasted off across space!
"Yippee!" whooped Grandma. "Let's find new worlds . . ."
". . . and meet new friends!" cried Jakob.
And the Space Train sped off so fast,
the stars looked like streaks in the sky.

# JAKOB'S LOG
## *03::02::2085*
## THE SPACE TRAIN

**Inventory 118:**

1 Boy (me)

1 Grandma

1 Robot chicken (Derek)

1 ToolBot (less grumpy)

3 Galaxies, 39 planets
visited

18 Comets chased

5 Star whales met

120 Passengers

120 New friends (yes!)

1,000,000,000,000
new adventures
to have!

I met
a dinkybop!

My new friends
on the Moon of Elm